HITTY'S TRAVELS

Ellis Island Days

ELLEN WEISS

ILLUSTRATED BY BETINA OGDEN

ALADDIN PAPERBACKS

New York   London   Toronto   Sydney   Singapore

First Aladdin Paperbacks edition August 2002
Text copyright © 2002 by Ellen Weiss
Illustrations copyright © 2002 by Betina Ogden

Aladdin Paperbacks
An imprint of Simon & Schuster
Children's Publishing Division
1230 Avenue of the Americas
New York, NY 10020

Also available in an Aladdin library edition

Designed by Debra Sfetsios
The text of this book was set in Celestia Antiqua.
Printed in the Unites States of America

2 4 6 8 10 9 7 5 3 1

The Library of Congress Control Number for the Paperback Edition: 2001053442

ISBN 0-689-84945-1

CHAPTER ONE

My Journey Begins

Imagine, dear reader, that you were alive in the winter of 1908. Imagine yourself standing in the middle of Mulberry Street in New York City. The last snowfall would have been turned to a freezing, sooty soup by a thousand boots and cart wheels. The street would have been jammed with carts. You'd have seen the ragman, the egg man, the knife grinder, the ice man, calling out their wares. You'd see groups of children running up and down the street in shouting swarms. All around you, you would have heard the musical sounds of the Italian language. For this neighborhood was called Little Italy.

And if you had looked up—all the way up to

the fifth floor of the building across the street—you would have seen something interesting. You'd have seen a small wooden doll, propped in the window. This doll would be gazing out over the street, as if wondering how in the world she'd gotten to this place.

That doll was me: Hitty, short for Mehitabel. And I was indeed thinking about the incredible story of how I had arrived at 154 Mulberry Street. For it had been one of the strangest journeys of my life.

Just six months before, I had been shut up in a glass case in a toy store. I was surrounded by tops, India-rubber balls, and dolls. A large hand-lettered sign hung over my head. HITTY, it said. ANTIQUE DOLL, HANDMADE. PROBABLY CARVED AROUND 1820. THIRTY DOLLARS.

I had been sitting there for quite some time. Every now and then, a customer would ask the storekeeper to open the glass case and take me out. But thirty dollars was an awful lot of money at that time. I could not see how anyone would want to pay that much for a ninety-year-old doll. For thirty dollars, you could buy an entire wardrobe, including shoes and a coat.

But then a tall man had entered the store. Right away, he had headed for my glass case. After looking at me for a moment, he said, "I'll take it."

Though I found it a bit unsettling to be called "it," I was happy to be going to a new home.

"How do you know its name is Hitty?" asked the tall man.

"Look," said the shopkeeper. She carefully lifted my blue calico dress. "It's sewn onto her slip. See the red thread? Her first owner probably embroidered it."

My first owner. By now, Phoebe Preble was likely gone from this earth. But I would never, ever forget her.

"Can I ask where Hitty is going?" asked the shopkeeper. "I'm curious to know where life will take her next."

The man looked a bit annoyed. "Yonkers, New York," he replied curtly.

I did not know where Yonkers was, but it involved an hour-long carriage ride. At last, the carriage came to a stop. The man snatched me up from the seat. Then he stepped down onto the carriage platform at the curb. As he dusted off his jacket, I got my first good look around.

What a beautiful place I was in! The winding street was lined with large, stately homes. The trees were tall and leafy. And the view stretched all the way down the hill and across the Hudson River.

The heavy wooden door of the house swung open, and out ran a pretty girl of about seven. She had long, straight blond hair. "Daddy! What did you bring me?" she cried.

She stopped short when she saw me. "You said you'd bring me a doll," she said. "What's *this*?" Her bottom lip stuck out and her eyes narrowed. Suddenly, she did not look pretty any more.

"This," he said, handing me over, "is a very expensive antique doll. Its name is Hitty."

"It's old and ugly. Why didn't you bring me a new doll?" she demanded.

"This one is special, Louisa," he said coaxingly. "It's not everyone who gets a doll that's been around for ninety years. Anybody can get a new doll."

"Look at her! She's made of wood! I wanted a china doll! With real human hair!"

I listened to this, trying to keep my spirits up. But clearly I was in for a trying time.

Louisa's father was beginning to look annoyed. "Louisa," he said, "You asked for a doll. I bought you a doll. That's the end of it. Now go inside and play with it."

"It's a stupid doll," said Louisa. She snatched me out of her father's hand and marched into the house with me.

Inside, she stomped noisily up the stairs. Peering about as best I could, I got a glimpse of a comfortable, well-furnished home. The living room downstairs had an enormous hand-carved fireplace. The sofa before it was covered in a rich, maroon velvet. There were oriental rugs on the floor.

On the second floor, I was carried through what looked to be Louisa's bedroom. She crossed the room and we entered an adjoining sunroom. The light streamed in through the windows and hit a collection of toys that would have made any girl swoon. There was a magnificent rocking horse. There were shelves of brightly-colored books. And there must have been fifty dolls, one more beautiful than the next. I could see why Louisa was disappointed in me.

Waiting in the sunroom were two girls. They had clearly been playing with Louisa when her father had arrived home.

"Well, what did he bring you?" asked a girl with curly red hair.

"Just this thing," said Louisa. She flung me onto the floor in front of them.

"Ugh!" said the girl. "It's horrible."

The third girl bent down to have a closer look at me. "I think she's rather sweet," she said. "In a sort of an ugly way. If you don't want her, you can give her to me."

"You can just put that thought out of your mind, Victoria," said Louisa. "She's mine."

"Well, pardon me, Miss Snippy," said Victoria.

"Pardon *me*, Miss Give-it-to-me," retorted Louisa.

I lay on my back, looking up at the three of them. I had never in my life seen such unpleasant behavior. I could only hope that Louisa would tire of me quickly. Perhaps she would give me away, or have her father return me to the store.

"Let's play at jacks," said the redhead.

The jacks were taken off the shelf, and I was pushed to the side and forgotten. I was just as happy that way. The less attention I got, the better.

The game of jacks progressed with much squabbling. There were constant accusations of cheating. Meanwhile, from somewhere else in the house, I could hear the sound of coughing. It sounded like a child.

"Your brother's coughing again," said Victoria.

"I know," said Louisa. She made a face. "It's so boring."

"Do you think we should help him?" asked the redhead.

"Don't be an idiot, Edith," said Louisa. "The maid will go to him. Keep playing."

They kept playing, and eventually the coughing faded away. Someone must have gone to the child.

❧ CHAPTER TWO ❧

A Surprise Journey

From then on, I sat on the floor in a corner of the room. Louisa must have decided I was not fit to share the shelves with her other dolls. I was completely forgotten. I could feel that a cobweb was growing between my head and my shoulder.

Louisa's friends came over often. There were a couple of other girls besides Edith and Victoria, but those two were the main ones. The three girls always spent more time arguing than playing.

I soon met the owner of the cough, as well. Every now and then, Louisa's younger brother William would come into the sunroom. He was thin and pale. "Can I play with you?" he would ask. "I'm bored." Then, as often as not, he would be seized by a fit of coughing.

"No, of course you can't," was the answer he always got. "Don't be ridiculous. And don't cough on us."

One July day, Louisa's mother entered the sunroom. This was an unusual event. In fact, I had never seen her before. She was a tall, striking woman, with her hair swept up in the latest fashion. She wore an exquisite white dress. It just grazed the floor as she swept into the room. Louisa, who was alone reading a book, barely glanced up at her.

"Louisa, my dear, I must talk to you," said her mother.

"Why?" said Louisa rudely.

"You learned about Italy in school last year, didn't you?" said her mother. "Well, we are going there."

"I don't want to go there. I want to stay here."

"I'm afraid we can't, dear. The doctor has ordered this trip. William is not improving. He needs the warm Mediterranean air to help him get better."

"Then send William to Italy!" said Louisa. "I'm not going!"

"Don't be silly, dear. We're all going. Besides, it will be very glamorous. We will be the envy of our friends. We will be away for six weeks. We're sailing on a beautiful ocean liner called the *Nord America*. And you'll adore Italy. It's a lovely country. We'll sail to Naples, and from there to the Isle of Capri."

"Yes, and no one speaks English there, and it will be so boring!"

I, for my part, was wishing it could be me taking this trip. One of my owners, perhaps thirty years before, had been a lovely girl named Alice North. She had taken Italian lessons the whole time I had been with her. I had absorbed quite a bit of Italian. I yearned to have the chance to test my knowledge. And I did love to travel and see new things.

"We're going on this trip, and that's all there is to it," said Louisa's mother. "You must simply get used to the idea." She turned and left the room.

Louisa threw her book across the room, where it landed with a crash on top of a toy drum.

Preparations for the trip proceeded in spite of Louisa's wishes. Great steamer trunks were bought, with wooden drawers and compartments inside. Deliverymen brought hats in hatboxes and fine clothing with cloth covers.

A few days before they were to depart, Edith and Victoria came to play. Louisa had piled up in one corner the things that she had chosen to take. There were two of her best china dolls and about five books.

The girls played cat's cradle, but Victoria kept eyeing me. Finally, she spoke to Louisa. "You're not taking the wooden one," she said. "Why don't you let me keep her while you're gone? I'll make her a new dress. You can have it back when you return."

Louisa's eyes narrowed in quite an unattractive way. Then she snatched me off the floor. "It just so happens, Miss Envious, that I *am* taking her. Just her, not even the other ones. What do you think of that? I know you want to get your hands on her, but you never will!" She crushed me to her chest.

"Fine," said Victoria. "Take her. I don't care."

"Fine," said Louisa.

I was amazed at this turn of events. Louisa was actually willing to take a doll she did not want, purely out of spite.

Well, at least I was going to Italy.

At last it was July 1, the day of our departure. An extra-large carriage had been hired to hold the family and all their luggage. Louisa almost forgot me, but at the last minute took me up roughly. "Well, Hitty, you're going to Italy," she said. "I'll bet it's the first time you've been any-where in your whole boring life."

If she only knew how much of the world I had seen!

The ship was waiting at the dock when we arrived. It was a huge white vessel, bigger than any ship I had ever seen. Rising high above it were two great masts, and two smokestacks. The sides were lined with rows of portholes. It looked like an enormous building on the water.

I had expected to see great crowds of people packing onto the boat, but I was wrong. We were to have very little company, it seemed. There was just a trickle of people going up the gangplank.

Louisa's father must have been wondering about the same thing. "Not many passengers, eh?" he said to the sailor who was taking our tickets.

"Not in this direction," said the sailor. "They're all coming the other way. Everybody wants to get *in* these days. There are only ninety folks going to Italy today, all in first class. When we come back, the whole bottom of the ship will be packed. There'll be over twelve hundred people down there in steerage."

"Ugh," said Louisa's father. "Immigrants. They're dirty and they smell bad. I'm glad we won't have to share a boat with them."

"Of course," his wife reminded him, "we *will* have them on the way back."

They both shuddered.

Because I am a doll who keeps her eyes open, I knew a bit about the world. I was aware that a flood of people had been coming to live in America lately. These people were called immigrants. I had heard quite a few customers in the toy shop complaining about it. "Foreigners," they would say. "They're ruining our country."

I always wondered about these people who complained. Had not their parents or grandparents once been foreigners too? It seemed to me that only the Indians had a right to grumble about outsiders.

We were shown to our stateroom. It was as comfortable as a living room. The furniture was heavy and carved. There were thick carpets and drapes. The beds were made up with brocade spreads.

"May I please explore the ship?" asked William.

"All right," said his mother. "But be sure to wear your neck scarf."

"I will, Mother."

"I want to go too!" said Louisa.

"Go ahead. Our cabin is number twenty-three. You can ask someone if you get lost."

Louisa had already dropped me on the floor, but her father stopped her as she was leaving. "Aren't you going to take the doll? After what I spent on it?" he asked.

"Fine!" she snapped. "I'll take the doll."

And so we were off on our exploration. The ship was enormous. Louisa took the lead, with William struggling to keep up. Up and down the narrow staircases we went, from one deck to another. Louisa carried me dangling by one hand.

We looked in at the dining salon. The round tables were covered in white linen cloths. Waiters were going about with carpet sweepers, removing any stray specks from the carpet. The next stop was the gymnasium. Sets of heavy barbells stood ready to be lifted by energetic passengers. There was a smoking room for the gentlemen and a card room for after dinner.

There was a sudden, deafening blast of sound

from the smokestack. "We're going!" William exclaimed. He and Louisa raced up to the deck, to wave good-bye to the crowd on the dock. It turned out that the crowd was only about a dozen people. But William and Louisa waved with great energy anyhow. William waved his neck scarf. Louisa waved my arm.

As we pulled out of the harbor, we were accompanied by two fireboats. "Look!" said William, pointing. The boats were sending tall sprays of water into the air as a grand send-off.

We were on our way.

CHAPTER THREE

Disaster!

Once the excitement of exploring the ship wore off, things quickly fell into a routine. Up at eight in the morning, a few "turns around the deck," as Louisa's father called them, then breakfast in the dining salon. The tables were set with fine china and crystal. Louisa was shockingly rude to the waiters, but her parents did not scold her. They were rather rude themselves, I thought.

After breakfast, there were all sorts of games to play on the decks. The ship provided balls, ringtoss, and skipping ropes. In the lounges, there were board games.

There were several other children on the trip. Louisa bullied them all. She set the rules for the games and then changed them when she felt like it. I noticed after a few days that the others had begun avoiding her.

After lunch, passengers would spend several hours napping or reading. The ship had a small library, stocked with popular books for adults and children. Long rows of teak lounge chairs were set up on the decks. A fluffy plaid blanket was folded and waiting on each chair.

Then came dinner, more board games, and finally bedtime. For the grownups, there was dancing late into the night to a live orchestra. I could hear the strains of music from the family's cabin.

By the time two or three days had passed, Louisa was restless and bored. She had explored every inch of the ship. She had played every game there was to play. She began to whine constantly. "When will we be there?" "It's so boring!" "I hate this ship!"

At last, after eight days on the water, we arrived. The port of Naples was very busy. There were several ships waiting to take on passengers. The docks swarmed with bewildered-looking families carrying bundles and suitcases.

We waited in the cabin for the luggage to be unloaded. "Tomorrow afternoon, we will sail for the Isle of Capri," said Louisa's mother. "Tonight we will stay at Parker's Hotel. I hear it is very nice. You can see Capri from the windows. And we will have time to do some sightseeing. Won't that be lovely? We'll go see the Royal Palace, and the Church of Santa Chiara, and . . ."

"Do we have to?" Louisa interrupted her.

Her mother looked taken aback. "Of course we do," she said. "We can't be in Naples and not see its sights."

"Oh, wonderful," said Louisa, crossing her arms angrily. "You can look at them if you want. But I'm not going."

Finally the luggage was unloaded, and we were off to the hotel. After a pasta lunch in the hotel restaurant, it was time to see the sights. Louisa's mother carried a parasol. The late-June sun poured down from the sky. It was baking hot.

"Let's walk down the Via Toledo," said Louisa's father. "I have read that there are beautiful buildings along that road."

"Yes, and elegant shops, as well," added his wife. "Perhaps I can buy a new hat there."

And so, off we trooped toward the Via Toledo. The city was magnificent—what I could see of it. Unfortunately, I was forced to look at it upside down. This was because Louisa held me by one foot. I dangled limply at her side, my dress flapping up in a most unladylike way. I did however get a good view of the cobblestone streets.

It was awfully hot. Louisa's hair hung in damp strings. Her face was flushed.

"Mother, will you carry my doll?" she asked in a whining voice. "It's so heavy."

"I have to look after William," her mother replied. "Surely you can carry one doll."

So on we plodded. Louisa's grip on my foot grew weaker and weaker as she trailed behind her parents.

And then . . . disaster! I felt myself slipping out of her hand, but of course I could make no sound to alert Louisa. I hit the cobblestones with a jarring thump. Louisa continued walking and did not even look back.

Whether she let me go by accident or on purpose, I will never know. I lay on the paving stones, hoping she would return. Surely she would notice soon, I thought. Surely she would miss me and turn back. Would she not?

I looked up at the sky. It was blue, with fluffy white clouds drifting across it. The sun beat down without pity.

The street was busy. For a long while, people simply stepped over me or walked around me. Twice I was kicked by careless feet. The second time, the kick was hard enough to send me into the gutter. There I was terrified of the horses and carriages that hurried back and forth. If a horse stepped on me, that would be the end of me for certain. And that was not all. Now and then, one of the new horseless carriages would come barreling along, blaring its horn like some angry beast. I was sure that I would be reduced to splinters at any moment.

After some time, perhaps hours, I found that someone was bending over me. It was a handsome young man. He had a handlebar mustache that curled up at the ends. He wore a brown wool vest over his shirt, and a peaked cap. His thick leather boots were covered with dried mud.

He bent closer to peer at me. "*Che cosè?*" he muttered to himself. "What's this?" I was very glad I had paid attention to Alice North's Italian lessons.

He poked me a bit, and then turned me over. Finally, he reached down to pick me up. But just then, a great two-horse carriage came rumbling down the street toward me. He jumped back, while I braced myself for the impact. The carriage came within two inches of my head, but did not touch me.

Before any other carriages could come, the young man darted back to the gutter and snatched me up. "Come with me," he said in Italian. "You will make Fiorella happy."

CHAPTER FOUR

The Little Flower

It was strange for me to be carried by a young man. I could tell it was strange for him as well. He was not sure how to hold me. First he dangled me by my foot, as Louisa had. Then he thought better of it, and changed to holding me over his shoulder like a baby. This was even odder for both of us, I am sure.

Walking quickly, he carried me through the streets. After many blocks, we arrived at our destination. He pushed open a heavy door, and we were inside some sort of office. Perhaps it was a bank. There was a long line of people waiting, and at the front of the line was a barred window.

A man with a green eyeshade stood behind the window.

As we waited, I tried to adjust to my new situation. Would I ever see Louisa again? Probably not, I thought. Perhaps that was just as well, though. She was such a disagreeable child, and she did not like me anyway. But what was this young man's plan for me? Only time would tell.

It took quite a while for us to reach the head of the line. The young man stepped up to the window. "My name is Marco Rossi," he said to the man.

"Marco Rossi," the man repeated. "And you are waiting for money from . . . ?"

"Luigi Rossi."

"All right," said the man. "Let me look." He began sorting through a large box of envelopes. "Rossi, Rossi, Rossi," he said to himself. Then he looked up. "Angelo Rossi?" he said.

"No, not Angelo. Marco. From Luigi. Look again."

The man looked again. "No, sorry," he said. "Nothing for Marco Rossi. Next in line!" he shouted.

But Marco would not leave. "I know the money is there!" he said. "I am not leaving until you find it!" He was speaking very quickly in Italian. I strained to keep up. "Look. My brother Luigi has sent us this money, for his whole family to go to America. I know it's there. He's been working ten hours a day, building roads, so he could send us this money!"

"Everybody has sent money for his family to go to America. But your money has not arrived. Next!"

"Look one more time," insisted Marco. "I've come a long way for it, and I'm not leaving without it."

The man behind the window sighed. "All right, I'll look. But it's not here." He leafed through the pile again. "Marco Rossi?" he said.

"That's right, Marco Rossi. From Luigi Rossi."

"Here it is," said the man, handing over an envelope. "It was out of order. Next!"

The man did not apologize, but Marco looked too happy to be angry. He opened the envelope as he headed for the door.

"It's all here," he said to himself with satisfaction. "The money, and the tickets for the boat. Now we can go to America!"

So, I thought, *maybe I'm going back to America. What a funny world this is!*

Marco carried me a long way through the streets once again. Finally, we reached a low building on the outskirts of the city. Tied up outside the building was a donkey with a cart. A small boy was watching it.

"This is for you," said Marco, tossing the boy a coin. The boy grinned.

Then Marco threw me into the back of the cart and climbed up onto the seat. I landed between two sacks of potatoes. Luckily, I was sitting almost upright, so I could watch the world go by. The countryside was beautiful and green.

After several hours, we arrived at a small village with fields and orchards all around it. The cart pulled up in front of a little house. It was more of a shack really, with a low roof and a broken, crooked door. A few starved-looking chickens ran about in the small dirt yard.

Before Marco had even climbed down, the door burst open and children began pouring out. "Uncle Marco! Uncle Marco!" they shouted. There was a girl of perhaps eight, and three smaller children.

A woman came out behind them. She wore a dark blue dress and a black shawl. "Marco! Did you get the money from Luigi?" she called to him.

"I have it right here!" he said, waving the envelope. "And the tickets. We leave in four days! Our ship is called the *Europa*. You married a great man. I have to say so, even if he is my brother."

"I know he misses us," she said. "We miss him, too. But four days! So soon! We have a lot to do."

"Fiorella, come here," Marco said to the oldest girl. "I've brought you something from the city."

"But how could you—" she began. "I mean, there's no money for presents."

He stretched to pull me out of the cart. "I found her in the street. Somebody must have lost her. She was going to get run over any minute. Take her, Fiorella."

The little girl took me from her uncle, very carefully. She looked down at me with wonder. "This is—a doll?" she said.

I looked up at her. She had black eyes, with long, long lashes. Her dark hair was done in braids. *Fiorella*, I thought to myself. What a pretty name. I tried to figure out what it meant, and then I had it: Little Flower.

She inspected my hair, my arms, my clothing. She lifted my dress and looked at my slip. "*Hee*-tee," she said, trying to read my name. "What kind of a name could that be?"

Her mother looked at me. "It's a beautiful name for a beautiful doll," she said. "Did you thank your uncle?"

"Thank you, Uncle Marco!" said Fiorella.

"If you're going to be an American girl, you need a doll," he said with a smile. "That's what American girls have."

"Let us see! Let us see!" clamored the little ones. There were two little girls and a boy.

"Carefully, carefully," Fiorella replied, holding me down so they could look at me. "I'll let you play with her when you're a little bigger, okay?"

"Okay!" they agreed.

Then the little boy piped up. "Can I play with her now? I'm bigger than before."

Fiorella laughed. "Not big enough yet, Salvatore," she said.

A low whistle was heard from the side of the yard. A man approached, dressed in the same way as Marco. He had an axe over his shoulder.

"Hello, Marco! Did you get the money from Luigi?" said the man.

"I've got it right here," said Marco. "Tickets, too. Now we can go to America!"

"You and everybody else," said the man sadly. "There won't be anybody left in this village soon. What will I do for neighbors?"

"Why don't you come too, Arturo?" said Fiorella's mother. "Just leave the fields behind. Who needs this life?"

There followed a long discussion, only some of which I understood. They were all speaking very fast and using some words I did not know. But they seemed to be talking about high taxes, greedy landowners, endless work, and not enough to eat.

"If my Anna wasn't sick, I'd go in a minute," the neighbor said, as best I could understand. "We can never get even two coins to rub together here."

"In America, you have to work hard, but you can make money," said Marco. "You can have a better life. Look at Luigi. He's already saved enough money to send for the rest of us."

"If Anna gets better, you'll see me in New York," said Arturo.

"And then I'll say hello to you in English," laughed Marco. "I'll say"—he cleared his throat—"Hallo, Arturo! How's you doin'?"

And everybody laughed.

CHAPTER FIVE

Honey Biscuits and Tears

The inside of the house was clean but rather shabby. It had two rooms. There was a kitchen, and one bedroom for everyone to share. All four children slept in a bed in a corner of the bedroom. The house was dark inside, and the floor was simply packed earth.

For dinner, there were potatoes, greens, and some scraps of cheese. "Mama, may I have some more?" asked Salvatore.

"In America, you can have more, my love," she answered.

"Then I hope we get there tomorrow!" he said.

That night, Fiorella took me to bed with her.

"I'm so happy I have you, Hee-tee," she whispered to me. She smoothed my dress. "Now," she said, "if you're going to be an American doll, you must speak American. I will teach you. I have a book and I've been practicing. I'm going to have to be the one who speaks English for the family. At least until we see Papa. Papa has been in New York for almost two years. He'll teach us all English." She sat me up beside her. "Now, pay attention. *Good morning. It is a nize day. Where is the badroom?*"

She furrowed her brow, trying hard to remember the words. How could she learn English from a book, I worried. She could not hear how it should sound. I wished I could help her.

"Did you get that?" she asked me in Italian. "It's a very hard language. But we'll learn it. *Give-a me two aggs, please. With tost.*"

Soon she drifted off to sleep, right in the middle of my English lesson.

. . .

In the morning, the preparations began in earnest. Fiorella's mother was already bustling about when Fiorella went into the kitchen, rubbing her eyes. It was just barely dawn. The younger children were still sound asleep. Marco was already in the fields, working.

"Fiorella, come and help me bake the honey biscuits," her mother said.

"All right, Mama. Just let me get Hee-tee. She has to watch and learn."

I was propped in a chair, and they began working on the biscuits. Fiorella measured twelve cups of flour into a big bowl. Meanwhile, her mother was at the stove. She was warming up six cups of honey.

"I got this recipe from your grandmother," Mama explained to Fiorella. "It's special for traveling. The biscuits come out very hard. You can take them on a long trip and they never spoil.

And there are no crumbs. No mess."

As her mother poured the honey into the flour, Fiorella stirred the mixture. Salt and lemon rind were added, and more flour.

Finally, Fiorella put the big wooden spoon down. "Mama, it's too stiff," she said. "I can't mix it any more."

"It takes muscles," said her mother. "You'll have muscles in America. From eating eggs and meat. And chocolate cake." She laughed as she took the spoon.

When the dough was mixed up, Mama put it aside. "We have to let it rest for a while," she explained. "We'll bake it tonight."

After breakfast, the packing began. "We can't take more than we can carry," said Mama. "The rest we'll have to give away."

Fiorella looked alarmed. "I don't have to give away my doll, do I?" she asked.

"Of course not, *cara mia*," said her mother.

"You just got her. Besides, she'll bring you luck. She's a lucky doll. I can tell."

What a smart woman she was! You see, I *was* a lucky doll. The old peddler who had carved me for Phoebe had said so. I was made of mountain ash wood, and the mountain ash, he said, was a lucky tree. And he must have been right. I had seen many, many dolls come and go. But I had been through incredible things, and here I still was.

Now there were decisions to be made about everything. Take the good tablecloth, or leave it behind? Take the copper pot, or leave it? How about the little rug in the bedroom? And the feather pillow? Whatever they did not take would have to be given away.

At last, there were three piles in the corner of the kitchen. One pile contained the items that would definitely be taken. One pile would definitely stay in Italy. And the third pile was the hard one.

The children were sent to Arturo and Anna's house with some of the things that had to stay behind. "Tell your Mama something for me," said Anna to Fiorella. "If she ever gets tired of America, and comes home, I will give her back all these things."

"I'll tell her," said Fiorella.

There was so much to do before they set sail. All the clothes had to be washed. The house had to be cleaned. And so many good-byes needed to be said.

The next morning, Mama woke all the children early. Marco was in the kitchen eating breakfast.

"Aren't you going to the fields today?" Salvatore asked him, yawning.

"No, not this morning," Marco replied. "This morning, we are all going to visit Grandma and Grandpa."

The whole family dressed in their best clothes. Fiorella straightened my dress and wiped a spot from my face. "Grandma and Grandpa are going to miss us a lot," she whispered to me. "You have to cheer them up, Hee-tee."

The walk was not a long one, but the road was dusty. My clothing was full of dust very soon, and so was everyone else's. Everyone carried something that was being left behind. Fiorella carried me and the copper pot.

The grandparents' shack looked very much like the one Fiorella lived in. As we approached, the door flew open. Out hurried a very old, wrinkled woman. She had a scarf on her head, tied under her chin. An old man stood just behind her in the doorway.

"My family, my family!" she cried. A tear was already making its way down one of the wrinkles on her cheek.

"Don't cry, Mama," said Marco, hugging her. "We'll see you soon. We'll send for you. You can be Americans, too."

She shook her head. "We are too old to be Americans," she said. "We talked about this already, when Luigi left. It's a terrible thing, to say good-bye to your oldest son. You go to America. We will be Italians for as long as we live."

Fiorella reached up and wiped the tear from her cheek. "I'll write you letters all the time, *Nonna*," she told her grandmother. "In America, I'll go to school and learn to write. When you get the letters, you can get the priest to read them to you. He can read, I think."

Her grandmother looked down at me. She smiled a little. "What's this?" she asked. "A doll?"

"Yes, *Nonna*. Her name is Hee-tee. Marco found her for me. She was lying in the street in Naples."

"She's very beautiful," said the old lady. "She will bring you luck, I know it."

"That's what Mama says," said Fiorella.

Now the grandfather bent down and gathered all the children into his embrace. "You be good, all of you," he said, his voice shaking a little. "Be good little Americans. Even if we never see you again—" He could not finish.

"We will never turn our backs on our homeland," said Fiorella's mother firmly. "We'll come back. We'll make money, we'll be rich Americans, and we'll come back in our own boat."

This made everyone laugh.

"And the captain will have a fancy braid on his hat," said Marco. "And the boat will be called—" He stopped to think.

"The *Fiorella*," said Fiorella, to even more laughter.

By the time we left, the grandparents had indeed cheered up a bit. But even I knew that it might truly be the last time that family would be together.

CHAPTER SIX

Steerage

It was still dark when the family awoke on the last day in Italy. There was very little left to do. The packing was finished, the house was clean. Three battered suitcases and four bundles wrapped in cloth were piled by the door. The biscuits had been baked and packed into a small suitcase. Nothing remained but to eat breakfast and go.

Arturo, the neighbor, arrived right after breakfast. He was to drive the family to Naples in the donkey cart. Then he would take the cart and donkey home with him. I'd heard Marco ask his parents if they wanted them. After some thought, they had decided they could not afford to feed the donkey.

"All ready?" Arturo asked Fiorella.

"All ready," she answered.

Everybody piled into the back of the cart with the luggage. Fiorella sat me on her lap. Marco sat up front with Arturo.

"Remember," said Marco, clucking to the donkey. "Don't feed her apples. They make her sick."

"I'll take good care of her," said Arturo. "Don't worry."

And so, we were off. We bumped down rutted roads, passing farms and villages, all as poor as the one we had left. When the villagers saw the cart piled with luggage, they stopped their field work and waved. "*L'America!*" they shouted.

"*L'America!*" Marco shouted back, thrusting his fist into the air.

The docks in Naples were even more crowded than when I had arrived. Three ships were lined up at the piers. Thousands of people, it seemed, were milling through the streets toward the water. They all looked very much like the Rossi family. They carried suitcases, bundles, rolled-up rugs, and featherbeds. Some of the women carried huge bundles balanced on their heads. When it was impossible for the cart to move any farther, the family climbed out. Everyone exchanged hugs with Arturo, and he left.

Everywhere, there were children. The older ones looked after the younger ones. Fiorella held me in one hand, and her little sister Annabella's hand in the other. Annabella held onto the littlest sister, Maria. Their mother held Salvatore and some bags, and Marco carried the rest of the luggage.

"Don't let go of Maria, even for a second," Fiorella said to Annabella. "It's so crowded. You'll lose her in a heartbeat."

"I won't, I promise," said Annabella. But I was

a bit worried. She was so small, and the crowd was so thick.

"There it is!" said Marco. "The *Europa*! Look!"

He pointed to the third ship down the pier. It was enormous, like the one I had come on. It was gray, and looked a bit the worse for wear. Its three great, grimy smokestacks climbed into the blue sky.

Slowly, we made our way toward the ship. All around us there were people shouting and children crying. We were being carried along in a sea of anxious travelers.

Some distance away from the ship, we came to a stop. There were too many people waiting to get on. A man in a sailor's uniform moved toward us down the line. He was looking at the people and their luggage. "Too much baggage," he said to one group. "You have to get rid of one suitcase."

He stopped beside a group of people who were ahead of us. "You can't bring that chicken," he said.

"But why not?" asked the woman holding it. "It's a good chicken. We'll need it in America."

"They won't let you into America with that chicken," he said. "I can't let you onto the ship with it either."

"But what will I do with it?"

"I don't know. I don't care. Give it away, or let it go. Just don't bring it on the ship."

"I'll take the chicken," said a man standing nearby. "I'm staying here. I'm just saying good-bye to my family."

The woman looked unhappy. "All right. Take the chicken," she said, handing it over.

The sailor continued on down the line. I could feel the whole Rossi family holding its breath. Would there be something wrong with their baggage?

The man walked past without a word. Everyone exhaled.

Slowly, slowly, the sea of people inched

toward the ship. Finally, we were on board. Marco handed the tickets to the ticket taker. "Third class," said the man, barely looking at the tickets. "Downstairs. All the way down."

What a different sort of voyage this was! On the way here, the *Nord America* had been almost empty. The only passengers were in first class. Now, the reverse seemed to be true. I did not see anyone who was not climbing down to the bottom of the ship.

We went down one narrow metal staircase, then another, then another. Fiorella, Annabella, and Maria were still making a chain. The crowd pressed us downward. The smell of sweat was growing stronger as we left the fresh air behind. The light, too, grew dimmer and dimmer.

Downstairs, there were more sailors waiting to show us where to go. One of them looked at our tickets again. "Women and children, this level," he said. "Men, one flight down."

Fiorella's mother looked panicked. "Marco, how will we find you?" she said.

"Meet him up on deck," said the sailor. "You'll be up there all day anyway. You won't want to stay down here."

"But where—" she began asking him. But he was already directing the next group behind us.

"I'll meet you up on the deck in a little while," Marco called back to her. He was already being swept downward with the men. "Near the front, okay?"

"All right," she called back. "We'll look for you."

Finally, we were in our room. Fiorella and her mother stood in the doorway and looked at it in dismay. "This is where we sleep?" said Fiorella.

The room held perhaps fifty people. There were rows of bunk beds, with little space between them. There was one hook at the end of each bunk for hanging clothes at night.

"Where do we go to the bathroom, Mama?" asked Annabella.

A woman who was arranging her things under her bed pointed to the left. "Out in the hall," she said. "There are only two toilets for everybody." She looked disgusted. "We are like animals on this boat," she said.

Fiorella's mother sighed. "Well, it's only for a little while," she said.

There were two bunks for the five of them. Fiorella and her mother would share the top one, and the three little ones the bottom.

"I'm not going to let Hee-tee out of my sight for a minute," Fiorella told her mother. "I'm afraid someone will take her." She looked around her worriedly. I became afraid, too, that I would be taken. I did not think I could bear another accidental change of owners so soon.

"We'll just have to do the best we can," said her mother.

"I have to go to the bathroom," said Annabella.

"All right. We'll go find the bathroom, and then we'll find Marco up on the deck."

The line for the two bathrooms was very long. It was over an hour before we were up on the deck. It was already crowded with people.

"There he is!" shouted Salvatore. "I see him!"

As we reached Marco, we heard shouts. Sailors were threading through the crowd. "*Chi non e passeggero, a terra!*" they called out. "All ashore that's going ashore!"

The people who were saying goodbye to family members scrambled for the gangplanks. Then the great horn hooted once, twice, three times. The ship began to glide smoothly out of the port of Naples.

CHAPTER SEVEN

Up and Down

I am sorry to report that our departure was just about the only smooth part of the trip. In all my travels, I had never seen such rough seas. We hit two separate storms, which sent the ship pitching horribly. The ship plunged and pitched, up and down, up and down. Sometimes it felt as if we were climbing a mountain, and then being hurled off the top. I was afraid that the ship would break apart from the stress.

Everyone was seasick. Most of them, I learned, were farmers and had never been on a boat before. This was a very bad introduction.

In the daytime, when the weather was decent, all the third-class passengers jammed onto an upper deck. The seasickness, they all said, let up a bit up there. It was good to breathe the salt air. And if they were going to lose the contents of their stomachs, it was much tidier to do it over the side. It made me very glad I was just a doll, and could not feel as they did.

The immigrants did not have much in their stomachs in any case. Meals for the steerage passengers aboard the *Europa* were a dismal affair. Three times a day, enormous buckets of soup or watery stew were brought up to the deck. Great tin dishes were passed out to groups of five or six people. Every person got a spoon, usually dirty. Each group sat on the deck and shared its dishful. There was often bread as well, but it was moldy. It seemed that the passengers were given enough food to keep them alive, but no more. Even the drinking water tasted dreadful, Fiorella said. "I don't know if the food is making me sick, or the boat," she moaned.

"Does it matter?" said Marco. He looked green.

I was very worried about Maria, the littlest one. I did not see her put one bite into her mouth for the first week. She looked thinner and thinner, and was completely silent. The family ate their biscuits between meals to stretch the meager portions. But Maria would not eat anything.

The nights were very bad. It was never quiet in our room. There were always babies crying, or children whimpering. Sometimes even the grown women awoke gasping or shouting from nightmares. The ship pitched and rolled. I lay in Fiorella's arms, waiting for morning. At least in the daytime we could be out in the air.

The trip took almost two weeks, much longer than the trip from New York had. By the last night, everyone looked half dead. Fiorella had managed to coax a few spoonfuls of soup into Maria, but she looked dreadful.

Then, one bright morning, a cry went up

from the front of the ship. It was just one word: "*L'America!*" The word traveled through the crowd like something alive. It was whispered. It was shouted. It was almost like a prayer.

"Come!" Marco called to the family from the railing. Everyone on the ship was rushing to the right side of the boat. But the children slithered through the crowd to join their uncle. "Look! It's beautiful!"

Even though I'd had the good fortune to be born in America, I was still very moved. It was indeed beautiful. The harbor, full of big ships and small boats, sparkled in the sunlight. There were green, bountiful farms on both sides of the Hudson River. And there, almost close enough to touch, was the most wonderful thing of all: the Statue of Liberty. Somehow, I had managed not to see her when I sailed out with Louisa's family. We must have been looking the other way.

She looked serenely over the water, as if to

say, "It's all right. I'll protect you now." Her crown shone in the sun, and her torch climbed to the sky. A hush fell over the crowd on the ship. Many people cried, even big strong men.

Just to our left was a small island in the middle of the harbor. A group of buildings sat on it. "I've been there before," said a man near us. "That's the Island of Tears. We all have to go through there before they will let us into America. That's where they decide who gets in. Some people, they don't let in. Some people have to stay on this island for a long time. Some people have to turn around and go home. Children, even."

"Who doesn't get let in?" asked a woman beside him.

"Anybody with a disease. Anybody they think is feeble-minded. Anybody who can't walk. Anybody with no money, or not enough. A million things. They look at your eyes, your lungs, your heart, your pockets."

A wave of fear passed through the travelers. I saw Fiorella's mother look fearfully down at Salvatore's right eye. It had become runny during the trip.

"We'll just wipe it clean, Mama," said Fiorella with determination. "They won't see it. They can't turn him back. They just can't."

The ship, guided by a tugboat, finally pulled in at the pier. We were beside two other ships that had just arrived. Immediately, the people with cabins of their own, the lucky ones, got off. We had not seen them for the entire trip. They had their own world on the upper deck of the ship. Now they tried not to breathe in as they passed by the crowds of steerage passengers.

When they had left, a sailor climbed up onto a hatchway above the crowd. He carried a megaphone. "Everyone must wait here," he said. "Ferry boats will be coming to take you all to Ellis Island. That's where they inspect you before they let you into America. So get your belongings from downstairs. It will be a while before you can get off the ship."

We were so close, but so far! If we could have simply gotten off the boat, we would all be in New York, free to go.

"Papa is right down there," said Fiorella, pointing to the city.

"We'll see him soon," said Marco. "Don't forget, he had to do this too."

Finally, we got onto a small wooden ferry. The ferry had been going back and forth for hours, taking people off the ship. The ride to the island took only a few minutes. No one spoke. I could feel the dread that moved through the crowd. Every little while, Fiorella or her mother would wipe Salvatore's eye with the corner of her head scarf.

Once on the island, we were herded into a large building. The first stop was a baggage room on the bottom floor. "You can leave your baggage here!" shouted workers in several languages. "You don't have to take it with you!" But I noticed that not many people seemed willing to part with the only things they owned in life. The heavy suitcases and bundles were dragged along. Fiorella held on to me fiercely.

After a little while, something amazing happened. Workers began moving about the crowd, passing out food. There were sandwiches, fruit, cookies, and milk. The immigrants took the food gratefully.

"This is incredible!" said Marco, chewing on a ham sandwich. "This is like the food of the gods! This is the best thing I ever tasted!"

"America!" said a man beside him, with a broad grin. He did not speak Italian, but this was a word they both knew.

Now a ticket was pinned to the clothing of each immigrant. The workers filled in each person's name, age, home city, and destination in America. They used the ships' logs to find all this information.

Next we climbed a long, wide staircase. When we reached the top, there were doctors waiting. Each one carried a piece of chalk. It was time for the dreaded medical inspection.

Maria had fallen asleep on her mother's shoulder. A doctor signaled that she had to be put down. He wanted to make sure she could walk. Groggily, she tottered along. This seemed to satisfy him.

There were doctors looking at everything. Doctors with stethoscopes, listening to hearts. Doctors looking into ears. Doctors inspecting scalps and tongues. I noticed that for every few people they looked at, the doctors would write a chalk letter on someone's coat. Some of the letters I could figure out, some I could not. L meant "lame." H meant "heart." S meant either "skin" or "scalp," I thought. Some people got an X, and I could not imagine what that was. The people who got chalk marks were separated from their families and taken somewhere else. Sometimes they were adults, sometimes children. It was a terrible thing. Nobody knew what this meant. Would the families see their loved ones again? Would they be sent back home? Everyone cried. I felt like crying too.

It was time for the eye examination. Marco had given Salvatore's eye one last furtive wipe on the stairway. But would that be enough? I could hardly bear the waiting and fear.

The eye exam was not pleasant. Each person's eyelids were turned inside out by the doctor. To do this, he used a buttonhook. This was a tool people usually used to fasten the loops around shoe buttons. I could scarcely watch. Luckily, it was over very quickly.

The family tried not to look too worried when the doctor got to Salvatore. He looked into the boy's left eye. He looked at the right eye. He bent down to look harder.

He thought about it. Then he flipped Salvatore's eyelids right-side-out and sent him on.

The whole family sagged with relief. Fiorella went so limp for a second, she almost dropped me. But she quickly recovered, and we walked on.

Next, we were all herded into a tremendous room. It was an amazing scene. There were thousands of people in it, waiting in lines. Iron railings separated the lines. As we got closer, I became aware of all the different languages being spoken. Our ship had come from Italy, but clearly there were ships coming in every day from all different countries. I recognized Italian, Russian, and German, but I did not begin to know what most of the other languages were.

Then came the endless waiting. Go wait on this line, someone said. No, this is the wrong line. Go wait on that line. No, you have to start all over. The immigrants shuffled along, too tired and frightened to protest. The children were completely worn out. Maria slept in her mother's arms. Annabella was carried by Marco. Salvatore simply lay down on the floor. He used the rolled-up rug as a pillow.

At last, after hours of standing and waiting, the family reached a desk. Behind it was a man with a great big book. Sitting beside him was a woman.

"Name?" said the man.

"*Nome?*" translated the woman.

The two adults gave their names, and the names of the children. But before her mother could say her name, Fiorella stepped forward. "My name is Fiorella Rossi," she said clearly, in English.

"Good girl!" said the woman. "How old are you?"

"I am eight old," said Fiorella.

"Eight years old," the woman corrected her. "Very good. You'll do well in America."

"Thank you," said Fiorella, smiling very hard.

"And who is this?" the woman asked, pointing to me.

"Hee-tee," Fiorella replied. She showed the woman my name on my slip.

"Hitty," the woman said.

"Hitty," Fiorella repeated carefully. "Hitty."

After that, there was a long list of questions to be answered by the grownups. All the questions were translated into Italian by the woman. "Where are you going to live?" "Do you have family here?" "Who paid for your passage?" "How much money do you have?" "Do you have a job waiting here?"

Who knew what the right answers were? I could tell that Marco did not. Did they have enough money? Was it better to have a job, or not? There was nothing to do but tell the truth and hope for the best.

It seemed that the truth was good enough.

For when all the questions had been answered, the man stamped their passports with a loud thud. The Rossi family was free to go.

We had been on Ellis Island for seven hours. Now we made our way down a long hallway. At the end was a door. A sign on it said, PUSH FOR NEW YORK.

A very large ferry was waiting for the lucky, weary travelers who came out that door. This was the very last leg of a long journey. Fiorella stood beside her mother at the railing of the ferry, looking at the city. It was nighttime already. All the gas lights of the city were lit. It looked grand.

Next to Fiorella was a small blond girl. She pointed at me. "*Was ist das?*" she asked. I recognized this language as German.

Fiorella held me out to the girl, who took me carefully. She held me for a moment, kissed my nose, and handed me back. "*Danke*," she said.

"*Prego*," Fiorella replied. "You're welcome."

In ten minutes, the Ellis Island ferry pulled in to the terminal in New York. The crowd spilled out, ready to begin their new lives. Fiorella and the adults took firm hold of the smaller children and the baggage. They walked down the ramp and into America.

And then Fiorella let out a yell. "Papa!" she shouted. "Papa! Papa!"

Across the room, a man stood waiting. He looked very much like Marco, but with an even bigger mustache. He ran to join his family. Fiorella flew into his arms first. There was so much hugging! There was a great deal of crying, too.

"Have you been waiting long for us?" his wife asked him, wiping her eyes.

"Just since yesterday," he said. "I wasn't sure when the ship was coming in."

Maria and Annabella hung back a little.

"You don't remember your Papa, do you?" said Marco.

They shook their heads shyly.

"You'll get to know me again soon," their father said. He reached into his pocket, and out came four candies, one for each child. "Salt water taffy," he said. "American candy." The children smiled.

"And the apartment . . . ?" asked his wife.

"All ready and waiting," he said. "Four rooms, right on Mulberry Street. We have to walk up four flights. And we share the apartment with the Gambale family. But they're good people. They have children waiting to play."

Their father scooped up Maria, Annabella, and a large suitcase. "And now, let's go," he said. "Tomorrow, you'll all start learning to be Americans."

And tomorrow, I thought, I would begin my new life in my old country.

About the Journey to America

The United States is often called a great melting pot. Its people come from every corner of the world. Some were brought here as slaves. But many others came to escape poverty or to flee oppression. Those people saw America as the land where anyone who worked hard could have a better life. This has been true since its earliest days.

Toward the late 1800s, though, the steady flow of newcomers started turning into a flood. Suddenly, it was easier to make the trip, thanks to the invention of the steam-powered ship. Wooden sailing vessels had taken three months to cross the Atlantic. They could not hold many people. But the new steam ships were first made of iron, and then steel. They could carry thousands of people. And the journey now took only about two weeks. The shipping companies fought with each other for passengers. The numbers of immigrants grew and grew. It reached a peak in 1910, when over a million people moved to the United States.

Italians were the largest group of immigrants by far. Most of them came from southern Italy. Life was very hard in this part of the country. There were mainly farms, but the people who farmed the land did not own it. This system kept them poor, and there was no hope of things getting better. In America, there was plenty of work for them.

Ellis Island sits in the middle of New York Harbor, less than a mile away from New York City. Between the years of 1892 and 1954, when it finally closed, about 90 percent of all immigrants came to the U.S. through its doors. Now, over one hundred million Americans—almost half the country—can trace their families back through Ellis Island.